Entangled in Domesticated Love

MIA W. JONES

Redbaby Publishing, Inc.

ENTANGLED IN DOMESTICATED LOVE

Book cover design by Shavar Sandler
Published by Redbaby Publishing, Inc., Clinton, MD 20735

Author's Note: This dramatization is based on actual events lived by Mia W. Jones. Names of several individuals depicted in this manuscript have been altered. The recollection is based solely on her interpretations of the events as they occurred

ISBN 978-1-952163-02-9 Paperbook
ISBN 978-1-952163-03-6 eBook

First Printing, 2020

CONTENTS

| 1 |

Dedications

First and foremost, thank you to my Heavenly Father who continues to shine his light, love, and grace upon me.

To my earthly Father, Willie Jones Jr. Thank you for being here and standing beside me through this process. I know it was not easy but, rest assure the best is yet to come.

To William "Chris" Monroe, My Knight and Shining Armor, The Love of My Life. I am so happy and elated to be your Queen. You are everything that I ever hoped for and more. I would not trade you for the world, my King. Thank you for the past, present and future. XOXO #Mr&MrsRight

Donnell Jr., Caleb, Mya you are my heartbeats, I apologize that mommy subjected you to this type of pain. I am glad now that I can allow you to see that there is true love out in this world for everyone. Make sure you never settle for anything less than what you desire. I love you always and forever.

To my three aces, Veronda, Denise and LaSandra, I love you chicks so much. Every phone call, all of my cries and tears that I shed, and you guys listen. I appreciated it from the bottom of my heart. Thanks for always being there.

To Yolonda McCoy, you are a true gem. For those times I needed you, you were there. I cannot thank you enough.

To the late Barbara Sampson thank you for being the best mother-in-love and best friend a woman could ever ask for.

Apostle and Prophetess Staton, thank you so much for allowing us to come in and be a part of your life. Your kindness, love and support will never be forgotten.

To Mrs. Tina Broadwater and family, Ms. Regina Holiday and family, and Mr. Scott Graham and family, you all are God sent. Thank you for the love, assistance and push I needed to continue going.

To the Dove Center in Garrett County, Maryland, I cannot thank you enough. You were there for me through some of my darkest moments. You continued to push me through my pain, and I am grateful because my life is now in the direction, I want it to be.

To Garrett County Memorial Hospital, the doctors and nurses that worked on me day and night, I just want to thank you so much for taking care of me. I would not have made it without your dedication and care. Bless you all!

To my Garrett Co Church Family Loch Lynn Church of God /Pastor Cindy Ackerman/The Children Foster Mother, God Bless You all. I really appreciated every call, drop in, help with my babies and everything else you have ever done for us.

To Prophetess Jaqueline Cade, in meeting you I found the strength to tell my story. Thank you for introducing me to Jones Harwell, who through her tender pushing guided me through every conversation, every memory to bring you this written word, my story.

In writing this, I have found a new peace. I finally know what it is to be in a loving relationship and be happy. My focus has become clearer and sharper. With a newfound strength, I am determined to carve out a better, more successful journey for me and my children.

For those of you who have gone through it, I know you understand the struggle, the pain and heartache. And for those of you who are going through it, may it give you courage to seek help and walk away.

| 2 |

Preface

When No One Wins at the Game of Love

In most games, whether one on one or teams, there can be only one winner. The winner either scored the most points runs the fastest or finishes in first place. Then the winner is rewarded or maintains a perfect record. Until the next contest the winner has bragging rights. The loser, on the other hand, bows in defeat. It is not always easy, but the loser accepts his fate and prepares for the next opponent. During preparation, the loser makes sure that the same mistakes are not made. In the game of love there should only be two players. The rules are simple love one another unconditionally, be loyal and above all never forsake one another by seeking the arms or attention of another. Usually this game has no losers. Everyone is supposed to win at the game of love. The prize is tremendous. Even a life of forever after is possible. All in of love the name of love the two know no defeat. Well let's switch this episode a bit. What happens when there are no winners? Is there a reward when both parties lose? Usually the sting of defeat is meant for one but now we have two losers. Losers of love life and living. Lost in mind body and soul. Wanderers of all that existed in a blissful setting. Losers who sought refuge elsewhere other than with the one they were with. Only to be left lost and alone no future some loyalty trust and love for each other is gone. Losers who have made only made the decision that caused brokenness sadness and despair. Why cause such hurt to the one you so called loved? Why is it that love leaves us? Is love just a combination of emotions that can potentially fade away overtime? These questions are just a few that will plague the minds of winners and losers of love. Since fear keeps us aware of our surroundings, would this be an option to help the unknowing be prepared? I mean who goes into a potential relationship preparing for a breakup? This is not practical, and it does not guarantee winners in the game of love. What of throwing in the towel? Does this act favor a loser in gives a quick way out of a bad situation? Maybe even waving the white flag. Could this be an early sign that there was nothing left to fathom? All courses of action to make things work have failed. You have reached a stopping point or a point of no return. Loser! Those last whom are not yet found. You both have given up. There is only an end to this game. No winner to take home the Crown. Just two of you who have nothing to give and nothing is received. The path of the loser is chosen. You go your way and I will go mine. Who needs you! Both are bitter and sore. Saying detestable things to one another. Becoming sore losers though neither wanted their fate. Wasted time, wasted energy, pointless agendas and the thought that we were meant to be united in matrimonial bliss. So fake! Now losers, pick up the pieces. Go on about your business. This game was not for you. You never followed the rules. You continue to look for fault. Never once did you consider each other's feelings or thoughts. You settled! Yes, you did! You settled with the idea that little ole you could make a change in one another. Selfish bastard! Now take your loser asses away from here. This game is not for the faint at heart, but for those who have established the right foundation and are willing participants. Now if you have what it takes to be a winner, let the games begin.

William "Chris" Monroe

| 3 |

Blank Page

| 4 |

Prologue

Red flags. Thinking back on it I should have heeded the words my brother-in-law Maurice and sister Maxine gave me upon meeting Latimore in November 2006. Maxine stated that her husband saw signs of his old self in Latimore. "Marissa," he warned me, "slow things down a bit. I am seeing red flags." But I was not listening. I was not trying to hear it at all. Latimore just asked Maurice for my hand in marriage and I was elated. Finally, I had found someone who loved me. Someone who would care for me and my son. Finally, my heart screamed, it is my turn for happiness. By January 2007, the downward spiral began. This was not love at all. This love cut too deep, scarred me way too much. This love cost me my pride, self-respect, time, and years. From 2007 to 2018, I endured more than I could imagine. I became too entangled in domestic love that turned out to be domestic abuse. In the end, I became a survivor, a conqueror. Never again will I allow anyone to make me a victim - **NEVER AGAIN.**

In the beginning

Me in 2015

| 5 |

My fairy tale ever after

It is October 2006. I have been divorced from Theo's father, Theodore, for a year. In my heart, I am still hoping for a reconciliation. My son is seven months old and we are living with my cousin. She is having a get together at her place and wanted me to stay and hangout. I am not that interested, but with nothing else to do I agree to stay. I ended up pairing up with one of the guests. I am clearly not interested in sex, partying, or anything else but I ended up getting caught up. Two dudes come in. The second guy, in a sweat suit, is dark-skin, tall around 6'1, and dressed in all blue and white; from the do-rag to Jordan's. The first thing I noticed about his face was his eyes. His eyes reminded me of bugs. They just popped out from his face. His whole gear was fly, but I did not care for the do-rag at all. There is nothing spectacular about Latimore. My first thought was, "Oh God." He is not handsome and clearly was not my type at all. But the brother had game, an intellectual game, and drew me in from the moment he opened his mouth. I let him know right away that this evening was not about scoring sex. He was cool with it and we spent the evening talking. In that instance the out-ward appearance did not matter. The conversation was deep, and I was pleasantly surprised. We exchanged numbers at the end of the night. I clearly enjoyed talking to the brother and wanted to see how it would proceed. It did not take long for things to escalate.

In less than a month, he is met my family. Everything up to this point is new. I never had a guy that opened doors for me, be courteous and downright chivalrous. Things are moving fast. At the first meeting with my family, Latimore asks Maurice for my hand in marriage. Maurice is sizing him up, tells me something about Latimore is off. There are too many familiar signs, characteristics that remind him of himself. He begs me to slow things down, but everything is new and feeling good, wonderful. I am happy. I am so happy I called Theodore and told him that I moved on. My exact words were "I waited for you for almost a whole year. I found someone and he found me. He even has a bigger penis than yours." Theodore replied, "okay, whatever," like he knew some inside joke that this relationship was not going to last.

I accepted his proposal and at Christmas I met Latimore's entire family, parent, siblings, and his in-laws. His family is nice, and his mother, Olivia seemed to like me right away. I immediately connected with his sister-in-law Irene. Something about her spirit made me trust her, feel comfortable like we had known each other all our lives. From the moment I got to their house, I kept going to the bathroom. I was not nervous or anything, but I had some issues going on and could not understand why I was constantly going to the bathroom. Irene was also curious as to why I needed so many bathroom breaks. Finally, Irene says to me on the down low "Are you pregnant?" In my mind I think she is tripping. Olivia was fixing Christmas dinner. Missing some items needed for dinner, we all decide to make a trip to the PX, as everyone had something they needed. Irene and me, made up some excuse so we could break away and get a pregnancy test. We were the last ones out of the store and his mom asked did we get everything we needed. I nodded we did. We got back to the house and made our way to the bathroom. The whole time I am crying, balling like a baby. I am upset with myself. Another baby was the last thing I really needed. Here I am in a new relationship, really wanting it to work and to better myself and now it is possible I am pregnant again. We set the kit on the bathroom sink and after a few minutes Irene confirms it. Yep, I am pregnant. His mother is ecstatic, everybody is happy, but I got the blues. I found it weird that Olivia chimed in and envisioned us having a boy and naming him Isaac. This totally blew my mind. Here she is envisioning my life, saying that she wanted us to have children and be happy. In that moment, it was like someone took a pin to a balloon, all the air just drained out of me. Here I am, newly engaged with an infant and the last thing I wanted was another baby. It never occurred to me that I could be pregnant – not now – not so soon.

For Latimore, at first, I think he was excited. He was the only brother who did not have any biological children of his own. All his brothers had boys and they even shared the same birth month. Our baby was scheduled to arrive September 1, 2007. Latimore's birthday is September 15. I wanted to get married in September, but Latimore with the assistance of Maxine and Doriene planned our wedding. We married on January 4, 2007. It was small and intimate. The gesture was sweet, but I felt let down. I wished that I had been involved in the planning. The bouquet was huge and gaudy; just plain ugly. The wedding dress was way too old fashioned and not something I would have picked at all. In retrospect, I really should have taken my time and not rushed things or went along with the flow. In a matter of four months I went from single with a baby to newly married and pregnant with my second child. I really should have listened to Maurice. Red flags started popping up often, like a seedy motel with a bad roach problem. I am starting to learn that he was not so solid, but a bully, a liar, and a con-man.

| 6 |

My knight in shining?

Four months into my pregnancy, my prince started becoming my demon. Subtle signs of abusive behavior began cropping up. Bright lights glaring at me the whole time, but I was walking around blindfolded. I believe in love and I believed he did love me. I consider myself to be an affectionate person. I have a bubbly personality. I am extremely animated; it shows on my face and in my talk. I like hugging and intimacy. Most importantly I like communication. Communication is critical in every relationship you have, regardless if it is between spouses, siblings, friends or even family members. Without it, you have no clue as to what the other person is thinking, much less feeling. Silly me, I am hormonal. My thoughts and feelings are all over the place. I am not trying to repeat past mistakes. Our marriage is new. Marriage requires work, trust and time. I was willing to work hard and take the time to really get to know my husband's wants and needs. I had made a commitment that I intended to keep. Early in the pregnancy I told him I was not sure if I were ready to have another baby. He told me that if I aborted or miscarried, he would kill me. I did not take that as a threat at that time; he was simply expressing his opinion. I understood with him not having any biological children of his own, this baby was important to him.

One day we were driving down 40 East having a conversation. I had to be around the sixth month mark. We were married and expecting a baby, and now we are out house hunting. I guess it was getting to be a bit much when out of the blue, he calls me a GOLDDIGGER (a woman who associates with or marries a man chiefly for material gain). That was disturbing to me. People often say things in the heat of the moment that they really do not mean. Calling me a GOLDDIGGER was simply wrong on so many levels. I never once presented myself that way and why in the world would he think that of me, his own wife? I am thinking *I initially did not want you but now I got you, and now you are trying to dog me while I am carrying your baby. Am I dealing with some mental issues going on with this man?* Everything is moving really, fast and I was just living in the moment. Then he had the gall to raise his hand towards me as to strike. I said, "for real, please I beat niggas down." Then I punched him in his chest and said, "what's up?" I did not get a vibe, or sixth sense at this point, a premonition of things to come. I coughed it up to a simple misunderstanding.

So, I am well into my second trimester and Latimore and I are on two different spectrums. We are not communicating well at all. He is not supporting me in the sense that I need to be touched, loved. He thinks us having sex while I am pregnant will hurt the baby. I am asking him to talk to me. I am a talker. If there is a problem, put it on the table and let us talk. Latimore, I found out, is the exact opposite and will not talk at all. He just walks away, after already causing damage on a mental level. Having you standing there wanting to know why. What was the problem in the first place?

Mind you, I am pregnant. Being hormonal is expected. They say each pregnancy is different – truth. I spent most of my first pregnancy in the hospital as my son was trying to come out of the sac. High risk pregnancies are hard, I think more so emotionally because everyone wants to have a risk-free pregnancy, free of drama, and have normal healthy babies. For the second time I am going through emotions again due to another high-risk pregnancy. Hello. I am asking and screaming for attention, for love. I really needed to feel wanted, safe and secure that everything was going to be okay. We are married. He said he loved me, so I am begging, asking him to talk and figure this out. I continue the discussion in hopes that he would just open up and let me know what he is feeling.

Our simple conversation is now getting out of hand. We are moving from bedroom to living room. Instead of talking like two rational adults, now we are arguing in the hallway.

The conversation starts to get out of hand and now we are arguing. Voices rising and the next thing I know, I am falling down the stairs. He pushed me. My mind is frozen, and I am saying to myself "He pushed me? This man who started off so loving and kind and gentle. HE pushed me!" I am mad. I am really upset. Rightfully so. I am sleeping upstairs, and he is sleeping on the couch. I should have held him accountable, but I did not. I was young with one young child and another on the way. I stay put. It is a Mexican stand-off in our house. Each of us in a neutral corner and the emotional abuse is horrific. No communication, no intimacy. At this point I am even going to the doctors getting prescriptions from my obstetrician to have intercourse with my own husband. What on God's green earth was I thinking? I shouldn't have to do that. This standstill continues for a while. A few weeks later, we get a phone call from his ex-wife Natalie asking if her daughter, Amber, can come stay with us a while. Latimore's marriage to Natalie lasted eight years, and from what I had seen to date, he was a decent stepfather. However, it did not take long for me to realize that when he walks away, he walks away from everything: the wife and kids. Subject and relationship becomes closed. He puts a period on it, period, exclamation point.

So, I tell Natalie I would relay the information to Latimore, and we will talk about it. About a week later we met at her house to discuss if her daughter, Amber, wanted to come live with us. After talking at Natalie's house, Amber decided to stay where she was. As we were leaving, I mentioned to Latimore that Natalie was pretty. A month later, we find out that Amber is expecting a baby.

Our baby, a boy comes a month early. I am alone. Latimore is home for the weekend, a free weekend from the reserves. It is close to me having Cephas, so I initiate us having sex. To me, it would help with the Braxton Hicks contractions and relax both my mind and body. He does not want sex at all. I am telling him it will help calm me down. He continues fussing at me to stop or he will leave. We continue the dance, jabbing at each other with words, and true to his word he leaves. All night I am in pain. Too much stress can escalate or intensify a situation, and I just wanted my body to relax. The next day I ready myself for church. The order of service starts with praise and worship (hymns) to usher in the spirit of the Lord. I love singing and giving service to the Lord. As I am stepping away from the pulpit after finishing our last song, the pain becomes excruciating. Bishop Shields and my sisters, Maxine and Doriene rush me out the church to my truck. They were pushing me into the truck to get me to the hospital. We get to the hospital and I do not know who called but they are rushing me to delivery. I am hooked up to every machine. The baby's heart rate is dropping. I remember them, the doctors, pulling, and Maxine is shouting "The cord is wrapped around his neck. Stop he is turning blue. The cord." My baby was turning blue. The doctors proceed to unwrap the cord from his neck and within a few seconds my baby is crying. What a beautiful sound that was.

Latimore was back on duty and does not see our son until a week after his birth. There was drama even over naming our child. Latimore, at 33, wanted Isaac to be our son's first name. I prevailed and named him Cephas Isaac. His mother, Olivia comes to help me for what we thought would be a couple of days. Her visit was not without drama. I sent my cousin to pick her up from the airport. The whole ride to the hospital she is complaining that she is going to "whip my ass" because I am mistreating her son. She has no idea that she is ranting to my cousin. My cousin calls and peeps me to the conversation before she gets to my room. I make nice initially and then proceed to inform her that it was not me but her son that has been mistreating me. I invite her to stay for a couple of weeks so she would be able to see for herself. We ended up having a good relationship. So much so that she called her daughter and suggested that I become a member of her wedding party. One of the girls dropped out of the wedding party and Bridgette needed a replacement. I volunteered to help out.

After all the months of insensitivity and coldness, we made our way back to middle ground, but the fire and intensity we had at the beginning of our relationship has changed. I could not quite put my finger on it but something else was off. Driving back from his sister Bridgette's wedding, I asked Latimore if he wanted to stop and see Amber's son. It was getting late in the evening. He says yes as it is not out of our way. We called and Natalie said it was okay to come by. I thought it would be a nice gesture to show that we were still supportive of Natalie and her kids. Natalie answers the door in a see-through nightgown. I'm thinking that he would be respectful and say "Hey, my wife is with me. Do you mind putting a robe on before I come inside?" I do not know if anything was said at all as he goes inside and stays almost thirty minutes; longer than I think he should have. The appearance, him standing at the door looking at her in the sheer nightie, to me just did not look right. I was able to put two and two together by his persona and charm, that it would be easy for him to be with another woman while still being with me. Just as quickly as I thought it, I brushed it off. No, Latimore would never do that to me; my man loves me.

| 7 |

This is a dream, right?

One of the reasons our relationship moved so quickly was the fact my cousin had put me out in November 2006. She seemed to think that Latimore had money and with the way our relationship was evolving that I would be better off. In the beginning he was wining and dining me. She felt that should have been her with Latimore. I was hurt. With nowhere to go, Latimore said I could stay with him and his roommate. That was really nice of him. I took him up on his offer. The plan was for us to get a place of our own. I was mesmerized and lost in the chivalry. I did not care where we were as long as we were together.

Oh boy, I really was all in on this feeling loved. I will say that the years were not all bad. From this union came two beautiful children, Cephas, and Muriel. I was naïve though. Deep down I did not want to believe that love felt like this. How could it be this bad; how could loving me make me fill so unworthy? I did not pay attention to any of the signs; the moodiness, the drinking and emotional blackmail. I was not thinking mentally, I was emotionally invested.

First, there was the ex-girlfriend, Melinda who lived a floor above us. I found that out by a young girl saying, "Hi Mr. Latimore," one day while we were leaving the complex. I casually asked him how he knew her, and he tells me that's Melinda's daughter as we were getting in

25

the car. The girlfriend that he just broke up with prior to hooking up with me. Everything was all good until the car broke down. Which car you ask? The car he was driving. I found out about the car when it broke down and then Melinda had it repossessed. Yep, title was in her name. Latimore said he was making the payments, but the car was in her name. I should have asked why.

Another incident occurred a few years later when he left his phone in the car while we were at Walmart. Something was telling me to look in the phone. I am not insecure at all, but women's intuition was telling me "look." So, I did. Here are all these pictures of a dark skin lady that I definitely do not know. She had on all white. It was so see-through; I could see her white underwear. If it looks fishy, then it definitely smells fishy. This man is cheating. Was this dark skin lady the one taking my husband's attention away from me and my children, along with his job and roundtrip commute of six hours daily? How am I supposed to feel? I am sitting in the car losing my mind! What am I doing? We moved from Maryland to Virginia. FINALLY, I am thinking everything is good OK and all is well now. But you know that anything can happen at any given moment. As they say I should have known better. I am walking around Walmart. Now I have my proof, physical proof that the cheating is happening. I walk in Walmart and found him in the center aisle. I stopped him in his tracks and asked him "who is that woman in all white on your phone that you could see her underwear." He said, "I do not know what you are talking about." And I asked the question again. He states nobody. Then I ask him a third time. I have three strikes you are out rule, so with me asking the last time, he had time to think up something clever. So, it goes a little something like this, "oh it's my friend Donald's girlfriend. He wanted to show me how she looked and see what I thought about it." I am thinking in my mind "WRONG!" I took my clear umbrella and hit him over his head with it, went outside and slashed three of his tires so he could not go anywhere. Then I began walking to Olivia's house. My eyes full of tears, this lady stopped to pick me up out of nowhere and took me the rest of the way. When I got there, she just held me in her arms and told me that it was going to be OK. I just could not say a word for about five minutes; all I could do was just sit there and cry. Eventually I talked to her while I called my sister, Maxine. When I got her on the phone, I told them both what happened. I am still crying while telling the story. After all I went through in Maryland and to move to Virginia to get this blow, I was just so fit to be tied. Once again there is a knock at the door. It was the police. I went to jail for assault. I was told that I could not be around him. Because his car was inoperable, he was at the house which caused me to be away from my children for two weeks until we went to court. Olivia kept in contact with me every day and she updated me on how the kids were doing when the kids were with her. I got to talk with them so that was a big relief.

For twelve years he had me twisted. If anything, I learned from him his favorite saying "**nothing beats a failure but a try**." I was tried and tried and in his mind he won. He got what he wanted. Latimore, the hustler, playing house, being a bully and playing single all in one fell swoop. For twelve years I tried everything in my power to make him love me. I fought through depression and weight gain. I made drastic changes to my body thinking I would be with this man forever.

Twelve years I took the pain, emotionally and physically. Through the moves, not only in Maryland, but even in Virginia. I kept the mind-set that when things got bad to just hold on to the good things to keep us together. But there were too many bad things, bad times. My quest to keep my fairy tale ever after was slowly becoming a nightmare, a fight for my life.

During the fight, it cost me some things. I lost custody of my oldest son. I fell into periods of deep depression and I became an abuser my-self; fighting Latimore for attention, fighting Latimore to keep from getting beat worse. The physical pains and illnesses I now live with daily. Slowly I began to fight back. What I put my children through, the pain and suffering they witnessed. Yes, I have regrets for staying too long. Marrying young the first time, I was determined this time to make the marriage work. In the end, finding the courage to love myself, along with doing better for my children played a large part in me wanting my life back.

| 8 |

My babies - my lifeline

During my pregnancy with Cephas, outside of the two incidents of physical violence, it was more of an emotional rollercoaster with him. No emotions, no physical contact. I felt alone and isolated. After having Cephas, the physical abuse became more frequent with no rhyme or reason for the cause of it. I was constantly walking on eggshells, pleading out loud and to myself what had I done to deserve this.

The abuse was becoming apparent to everyone who knew us. The arguments were so bad that one time, while his mother was visiting, she asked to go stay with his ex-wife until her flight home the next morning. He took her but it did not help that he decided to stay there until well after two in the morning. I was beyond hurt.

Latimore always thought I was cheating on him with my oldest son's father Theodore. I never crossed that line. Theodore would always bring child support money to me. We would talk about what was going on with our son, and how life was treating me. Latimore always thought in his mind that I wanted to be with Theo's father. My thing was and still is, Theodore is a great father. When it came down to any of his children and I made it known. Latimore, on the other hand did not want to deal with children after there is a conflict or he is no longer in a relationship with the mother. Theodore was always there for his son and Latimore seemed like he was envious that Theodore and I had a great rapport. We could still talk joke and play around with each. Theo's dad had this thing when he was giving me money, he would give it to me, then take it back. Give it to me and take it back. Then out of nowhere the money would be in his pocket and I would have to dig into the pocket to get it. We would joke, I would get the money and then leave. After an argument with Latimore for the thousandth time, in retaliation I told a lie that I had slept with Theodore. I admit it was wrong but to Latimore, it was his gold card to openly start cheating on me with other women.

One-night craving attention, before becoming pregnant with Muriel, I did something stupid. I had been asking and begging Latimore to spend some quality time with me. We have not been intimate for some time, and the conversations between us were slow and not exciting and vibrant like when we first met. Latimore decided to go out again. He went over to Maxine's and Maurice's place and took Maurice for a ride, instead of being with me. Everything and everybody seem to be more important to him than me. Feeling rejected and angry, I follow. I am trailing them with the pair of scissors, in the car on the front seat. In my mind, I am about to slash some tires. At this point, crazy you say – am I? Huh? This sister has had enough. So now I am following them. Next thing I hear and see are red and blue lights flashing and a siren wailing in my rearview mirror. I pulled over and the police officer is talking to me. She wants me to sit on the curb when I am already sitting in my car. I asked her "are you doing search and seizure." She said "no," and I said, "then I do not have to get out of my car." She goes to say, "Madam all I am trying to do is get you to calm down." I said I am calm. "Please," she implores, "I need you to calm down." I said "I AM NOT SITTING ON THAT CURB. No, I am not." Next, I hear "you're going to booking." I am furious. I ended up getting detained and released later that night for stalking, disturbing the peace and having a scissors in my possession (deadly weapon). Going to jail did not help my frustration or anger. It made it worse. Did he care? No, but he knew to stay out of sight when I came home. They released me from jail around 11:30-midnight. I walked home because I knew no one, NO ONE was going to come and get me. When I put the key in the door, I heard him get out of the bed. He put his shoes on and we met at the door. As he walked out there were no words between us. I knew if anything was said it was going to go down. By the way, did I tell you that he left my car at the spot where I got locked up to get towed? How about them apples?

We were living on North Montford, when one evening, after arguing all day turns into a brawl. It started out earlier in the day so minor. Once again, he does not care about my feelings. He is showing me that my feelings do not count. I am not allowed to feel a certain way about anything but the Latimore way. It is becoming so draining as he continues to put my feelings on the back burner. We kept going back and forth until he decides to finally leave. He had all day to walk away, step out to get some air, but no we keep escalating. So now we are trading blows as he is walking out. I have lost all perspective. I am running after him. While he is getting in the car, I am throwing stuff hitting the windows, hearing them break. I end up tripping down the stairs and break my toe. Latimore drives off and heads to Maxine's house. I head back inside to call Maxine and tell her what happened. He pulls up at my sister's house. I am ringing Maxine's phone. She picks up and I hear her saying "Oh my God. What happened? Did somebody try to rob you?"

"Maxine," I shout, "I happened to him" as she's telling me that he pulled up with all the windows busted on the car and he gets out looking like The Hulk, shirt torn and half on.

The beatings did not stop, and the mental abuse just kept coming. One time he punched me in my face on the left side. That punch ended up shifting my jaw to the right side, realigning my teeth. I went to the dentist and the recommendation was to either get a root canal every year or remove teeth. I ended up having a tooth permanently removed. I finally decided to leave. I went to a shelter with my sons. I was there for a couple of weeks before I started getting sick. I was dieting so I thought I was not getting enough nutrients. Wrong. I discovered I was pregnant again. I called Latimore the next morning and told him that we were having another baby. He was like "OK, but you left So what are you going to do?" I said I do not want to be here (at the shelter) having another baby, so I guess I am coming back home. I went back to Latimore because I did not want to have my baby in a shelter, and he did deserve to know. I went back to try again. I wanted my family to be whole.

With Muriel's pregnancy I had decided that I was not going to let Latimore hurt me, mentally, physically, or emotionally. If so, I was coming for him with a vengeance. My life was not a game. Latimore had deflated my emotions during my pregnancy with Cephas and it was not going down the same with Muriel. Due to the emotional rollercoaster he put me on carrying Cephas, I did not even care if we were intimate or not, but there were a few encounters. I chose to put my time and energy into caring for my two children Theo and Cephas. I wanted to have at least one good pregnancy because the first two were hell; so, this time I dolled myself up. Hair and nails started to be my thing, it was something that made me feel good and helped build my self-esteem back up. Then I started changing up the way I dressed; like turning over a new leaf it was on and popping. Then buddy, oh boy, I was turning the heads left and right. I just had to know that I still had it going on - from the "hey miss," horn honking, and "can I get your name and number." But the ones that meant the most to me was "excuse me Miss you look beautiful, or you are sexy as sunshine." They had to be the highlight of my day. To those men thank you for taking me to another level. I was never down in the dumps nor depressed.

Boy, I spoke too soon and became too confident. My easy pregnancy turned out to have an interesting turn, and now it is high risk for me again. For one I find out my husband had cheated and if your question is how did I find out? Let me enlighten you. Shorty, it was a mindblowing thing to me. I am finally building me back up mentally with the help of the opposite sex and this news tears me down. At six months my water broke, and I was admitted to the hospital. The doctors ran all types of tests only to discover that my own husband had given me a STD. When I found this out, I was livid. My attitude went from "zero to one hundred," really quick. This man put our baby's health at risk by putting his penis in somebody else! I just cannot fathom. I am trembling, shaking my head. I can feel my blood pressure rising. I am so angry. I cannot believe this!

The doctors did not give me the option to have the baby then. They informed me that babies can produce amniotic fluid from their urine. I was smoking hot. I wanted to check out of the hospital and beat the living hell out of him; like what in the world! I called my sister, Maxine, and spilled the beans. I knew the whole dang hospital heard me that day. Three nurses came in the room trying to call me down. I never had a STD in my life until then and my own husband gives it to me, the one that is supposed to love me, care for me, and protect me. I call and give him the business, all the information the doctors gave me, and first lie he tells me is I do not have it. Then he says maybe I got it from using somebody else's towel. My mind goes ghetto, "Nigga, Nigga, Nigga what you say? Are you serious! You got to be kidding me!"

The date is July 23, 2009 and my baby is ready to make her debut. I was ecstatic about having a girl. Maxine, on the other hand, said she was not buying anything until she saw for herself that the baby was a girl. She was tripping hard, she thought I was going to have another boy. It mattered because Latimore did not think we were having another kid. He did not want any more children. I was so happy that day, because that was my mother's birthday; it would have made that day just so more special. I just knew she was going to come on that day, but it did not happen. Latimore was there and of course my sister Maxine, and Maurice came with her, and we all waited while I was in pain. I am trying to have a natural childbirth for the first time. Yes, he was an excellent coach with helping me to breathe through the contractions so I was thought I really can do this until he starts falling asleep. Boo, Boo, Boo- so I began to lose hope and I asked for an epidural for the painful contractions at this point. I must've had my eyes closed for a long period of time and my reflex of opening my eyes was not working fast enough. I yelled out "I'm blind, I'm blind, I can't see" to Maxine. She said, "Gurl, shut up. Just open your eyes" and we all bust out laughing.

Slowly I opened my eyes, still laughing at my moment of silliness. For a moment it made me forget about the pain. Muriel finally comes on July 25, but she had to go to ICU for a week. The doctors told me due to the STD that she may have some issues, but you will not know until she gets older and start seeing signs, but just keep her as healthy as possible.

Almost immediately after having Muriel we start having conversations about not having any more kids. Latimore started the conversation by "you know we have a boy and girl and I think we should end having more children." I said OK this was fine with me for too. We got our little girl. I am married and though our marriage is not perfect I am thinking it was going to be for life. I did not think that doing this was going to cause me so much harm down the line, but it did. I did it because I loved him and I wanted to give him what he wanted but in return he had to do the same thing, permanent birth control which was a vasectomy. In October 2009, I got the ensure, permanent birth control. During this whole time my sister Maxine said "Marissa I don't think you should do that. You really don't know what the future holds." I do it anyway. I am still in love with him and the notion that we are going to work everything out and be a family. Boy was I ever mistaken.

| 9 |

I am not Mental, but He is

It was if my love was never enough. I stayed blind to everything because of loving that man. The beatings became so severe that I started hitting back, just to make him stop. I am slipping deeper and deeper into depression. I am gaining weight and just overall unhealthy.

This vicious cycle led to Child Protective Services being called after Latimore hit Theo while I was in the hospital pregnant with Muriel. Now there is a case, and Theodore is fighting me for custody of Theo. I ended up hospitalized looking at four walls at Mercy Medical Center, getting big as a house eating their yummy food. It was good. Maxine called and checked on me every day. Also, Latimore showed up when I asked to see my babies, Theo, and Cephas. It was always after he got off from work for brief periods of time and every time he came to visit, it seemed like it always frustrated him. I am thinking in my mind why in the world are you frustrated. I am the one in the hospital. No thanks to you. I can only think he could not handle the boys. One day it showed on their visit. He told Theo to get up on the chair and sit down, and Theo wanted to play. I did not mind because he was four and burning energy off. It would be good for him so when they get home, he could just give them a bath and put them to bed. But no, Latimore goes over to Theo and jacks him up by the shirt and throws him in the chair. Just as he was doing this a nurse walks in on him doing it and calls Child Protective Services. I was like what in the world.   Theo ends up staying with his father for the rest of the time I was in the hospital and yes, Latimore was guilty of abuse by CPS. I had no more visits with my kids while I remained in the hospital after that.

Losing Theo

Upon learning that we were moving to Virginia, Theodore became adamant about his son not leaving the state of Maryland. He gave me an ultimatum. "If you leave, then I would have no other choice to go to court and fight for custody. I told him, "do what you got to do," thinking that he would not follow through. The case pending against Latimore from CPS did not help matters. Why didn't I leave my husband then? I did not think to leave. I had one son by him and another child on the way. I stayed thinking I would have physical custody of all three of my children. The hardest thing I ever had to do was let my son go and live with his father. In the end I knew this was the best situation for Theo. I knew his father would be better for him. The pain though, I thought I was going to die. It was because of my first born that I am a mother. I knew the situation, with Latimore, was not good for us, but I could not bring myself to leave him. I still thought I could change him, love him harder, love him stronger and be a better wife. I was so foolish. In the end, Theodore made good on his word as the courts granted him full physical custody with me having joint legal custody.

A couple of weeks after the first hospitalization I still was not myself. We would still argue like cats and dogs even though the fighting died down, and that was due to him being near home. For me that was a plus, but it sent me in depression mode. Food became my refuge. I got big because I wanted someone that did not want me. Here I am in love with someone that did not love me. He was just there like a big piece of coal, doing little of nothing - it was just too much for me. Talking with Olivia about killing myself. I am contemplating running myself off the road with my car, all kind of crazy thoughts.

Conversations with Maxine and my sister-in-law, Irene finally convinced me to get help. They told me that I was worth fighting for, that my kids needed me. I was laying my life down for a marriage that was not working anymore. I was putting my marriage before my faith. I did not want another failed marriage. I believed that the only reason why he was there was for Muriel and Cephas. After a while even that was suspect.

I was stressed. I did not want to be bothered, so I decided to go to the hospital for anxiety and depression. I knew exactly what I needed because I felt it coming on, so they admitted me for a week or two. From that point on because I chose to get help for myself, and because everything seems to be so out-of-control, Latimore said I was crazy, I was bipolar. Having him tell everyone that about me that was the worst. I told the doctors everything that was going on with me. They kept prescribing things and they kept giving me drugs for something that I didn't know I had; but because Latimore had talked to the doctors and God knows what he said to them these types of things were placed in my mental health charts.

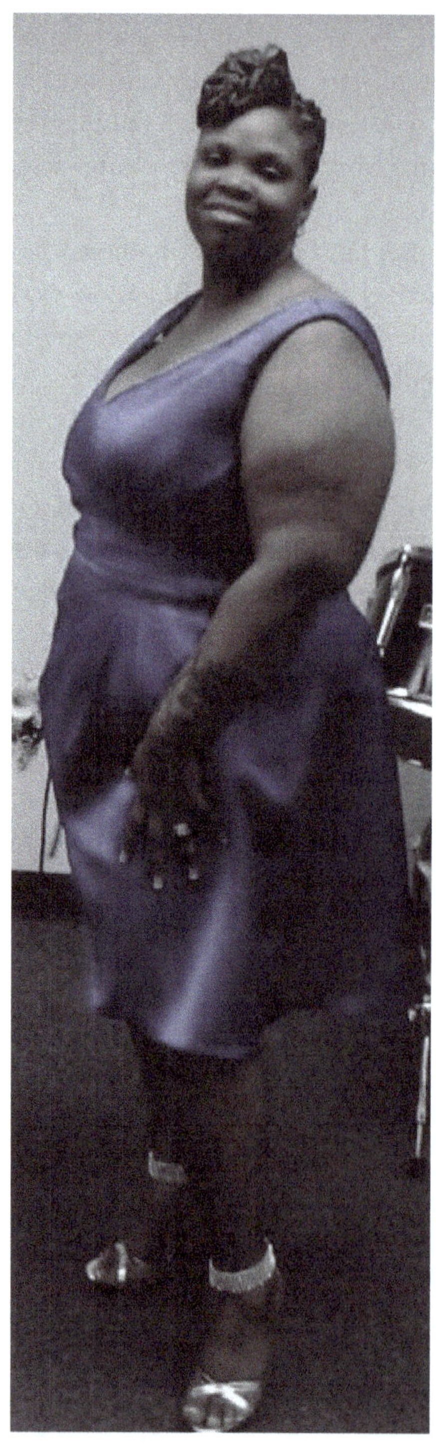

At my heaviest

| 10 |

Physical pains

I had already decided to hang in there if it was only for my children, but I really wanted to reignite those early feelings I had with Latimore. I believe in the institution of marriage; I honestly believed that we could find our way back to each other. Another step was getting control of my body back.

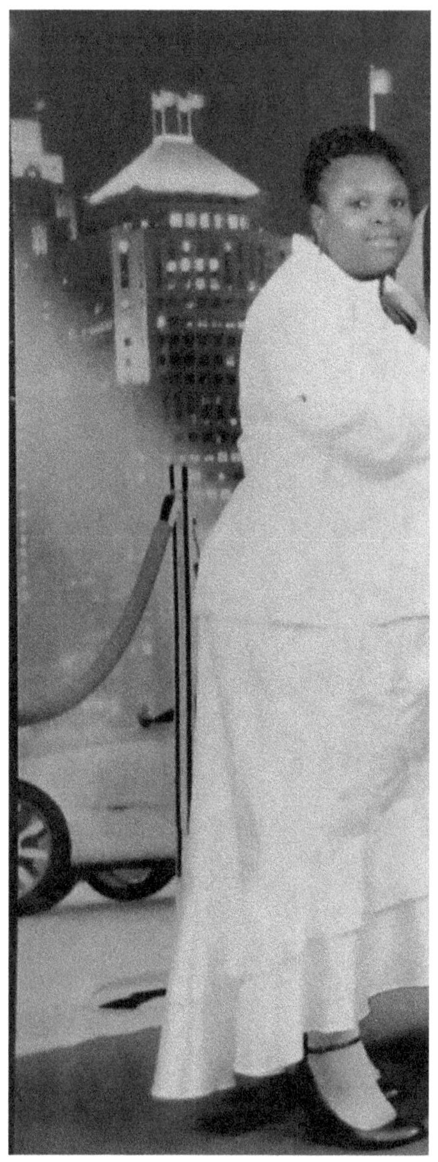

Before my surgery

I decided to have surgery to lose weight in March 20, 2013. Everybody is pleading with me to reconsider. Maxine and his sister-in-law, Irene are asking why I was so hell bent in doing it. Was it for me, they asked? Initially I did not do it for me. I want my husband to love me and care for me and want me. One day out of the blue I asked Latimore "do you love me? Do I mean anything to you? How do I look?" He stated, "I love you but I'm not attractive to you," which crushed me to pieces. I was already scarred from the mental, the physical and emotional abuse but to have that type of blow to my heart and self- esteem was low. Despite everything, I was head over heels in love with him it was not a thing that I would not do for Latimore. I did it as a way, I thought, to win my husband back so he would love me and look at me like when we first met.

Some of you might think my methods were drastic, but in the end having gastric bypass worked and is still working for me. If I made him happy, then everything would be alright with me.

Weight surgery done and on July 11, 2015, tired of having physical issues with the permanent birth control, I go back to my gynecologist. The visit discovered that my fallopian tubes had shifted. There's major damage from endometriosis. My periods are heavier and having sex has become extremely painful. The decision, after much contemplation and heartache, was to have a hysterectomy. Even if we were to decide to maybe have another child, it now was no longer an option. Here is another ordeal I am going through solo, without the full support of my husband. I am still doing everything for him because my world was all about him. And for a moment, our life was not perfect, but I am content with it.

Hindsight they say is twenty- twenty. Had I seen what was still to come, I believe I would have run faster than a roadrunner. However, I am still fighting for my marriage, fighting for Latimore's love and acceptance. I had no idea that the worst emotional and physical pain was still to come.

| 11 |

The Hustler

Slowly throughout our marriage I am learning that my husband is really a hustler and con man of the worst kind. When I first met Latimore, he admitted later that he and his friend were only coming over to use my cousin's place as a stash house for them to sell drugs. Like I said earlier, here was the first of many warning signs, red flags, that I just ignored.

We moved quite a few times during our marriage. At one point in our marriage, Latimore could find a steady job. We moved into a row house in the city of Baltimore and you know how that could be, insect infestation – roaches, mice, or both. I was such a clean freak. I was constantly cleaning just to make sure we would never see them. I got us a cat to help with keeping the mice out. One day I come home he is beside himself. A mouse appeared and he jumped straight up on the sofa. Seeing him jump on the sofa was the laugh of a lifetime to both of us that day. Who would have thought it though, one of my fondest memories is knowing that my 6'1 husband was afraid of a mouse?

During my pregnancy with Cephas, I helped him get a job with Mr. Kelly, who I knew through my father going to get his car fixed at his shop. With Latimore being the workaholic that he is I thought this would be good for him. But while working there, Mr. Kelly called and told me that Latimore had messed up a few times and he had to re-imburse his customers for the repairs. He was considering letting him go if it continued. I pleaded with Mr. Kelly to help us by keeping him on. Latimore had been in the military. I tried talking him into re-enlisting, but he did not think he would qualify due to a dispute of theft when he worked at Auto Zone. I convinced him to go re-enlist. Every day I would enter my prayer closet and pray that my prayers would be answered. God is good. Latimore was able to re-enlist in the Army Reserve. He was stationed at Aberdeen Proving Ground first and then later in Virginia. The kids and I were staying with Doriene, until a disagreement with my nephew about keeping the house clean. He kicked us out. We lived out of my car for almost a week. Latimore was on detail and was not available to help us find a new place to go. The Red Cross assisted and put us in a motel. It was not the best, but I made it as livable as I could.

After his duty was up at Aberdeen, he took another assignment at Fort Lee, Virginia.

This would his last station assignment in the reserves. After leaving the Army Reserve, he lands a job, a great job, working as a fleet supervisor for a limo service, which later leads to him becoming fleet manger. The job is in Sterling and we lived in Blackstone, Virginia. Things seem to be copasetic for the moment. I worked odd and end jobs at Dollar General and Hampton Inn while still being a housewife, keeping everything nice for him. I am thinking in my mind that I left my career as a medical assistant and a phlebotomist to allow him to advance. What was I thinking? Some might say that I sacrificed my own dreams, but what you do when you really love someone. You give them the best you got.

Played on my faith

We attended Spirit of Life Christian Church. Latimore grew up in the church. Both of his parents were leaders of their church at one point of time in their life. His mother was an Evangelist and his father an Elder. At the beginning of our relationship, Latimore saw my faith and I was able to get him to return to church. We are going to church and I genuinely believed that ultimately it would be faith that would bind us together and keep us bonded as a family. While living in Baltimore, we attended New Genesis Total Praise Center. Then we moved to Blackstone, Virginia and Bishop Harris gave Latimore an opportunity to speak the word. I was happy for him, excited because that was one of my prayers, that he and our family would continue to strengthen our faith. I thought Latimore had a word, a testimony, inside of him. He just needed the right time and opportunity to let loose. The opportunity came and his first sermon was called "The Three-Fold Man."

In this sermon Latimore broke down how "The Godhead," which is the trinity, was given to man to have the same physical makeup, image to be three-folds. Amazing. The sermon was so powerful. I thought he did a beautiful job. I was so proud and told him "I believe in you and knew you could do it. You are "Called." Just go through the process to minister.

I strongly believe that everything in life has a process. It is like giving birth to a baby. A woman goes through ten months of the growth process to form and deliver a baby. Latimore did not want to do that at all. He wanted to shortcut the process as usual. Bishop Harris was about to start a new leadership class at the church for upcoming minsters and deacons. Latimore was chosen to attend the classes to become a minster. Becoming an ordained pastor requires work, intensive studying of the bible and God's word. It does not happen overnight, but after months of learning and studying the word extensively. But boy o boy, after the sermon he preached, he went full blast on becoming a pastor. Now all the sudden, little by little, items are coming to the house; start-up items to build a church that he was going to open. I have always taken my faith seriously. It has never been or will be false with me. Preaching the word of God is a calling. It is taxing and requires much of those to follow and lead His charge. This became another bone of contention between us. I wanted Latimore to do this right. It became a constant battle between us because he was skipping the process. Understand me, the process to me meant becoming ordained. That is why till this day you will find Latimore saying, **"I am a**

Pastor / Apostle not called by man but God." What in the world? In my entire life, up to that point, I had never seen or heard anyone becoming a pastor without being ordained. This was the first time and it is called a bastard pastor and church. He even went as far as having an Apostle he met over Facebook to affirm him as an Apostle. Till this day he wears that title with deceit without regret. This same Apostle from Facebook advised him to leave me after everything that I had been through with him. Wow! Wow! This man! An Apostle, really, had never met me or had a conversation with me. He based his opinion on one-sided conversations with Latimore. Where they do that at? Most of the clergy leaders I know, always ask to have both members of the marriage available for counseling before making such a recommendation.

Nothing with him is never of any order. My bible clearly states that all things should be done without deceit and in order.

The day finally comes to open the church. I wanted to be supportive of Latimore and I was. I did everything, all the running around, to make sure that the day was special, especially for him. That is what you do when you are married. Even when you disagree on the methods, marriage is a partnership. Despite my feelings, I did not feel that this was done correctly, there was no agreement on anything, but I still supported him fully. The morning of the opening he stated that Bishop Harris laid hands on him and gave his blessing. Come to find out it never happened. I went directly to the source, asking Bishop Harris directly. Bishop Harris stated that Latimore was not telling the truth. No one to bear witness at all for such a monument event.

Latimore, always the charmer and salesman, manages to get Apostle Thompson and his wife, Prophetess Thompson, involved in his church. You see this came about because Apostle Thompson was one of preachers on the roster to preach on the same night as Latimore. Apostle Thompson spoke a wonderful word as well. So, afterwards they both talked and ever since then they had formed a relationship. Not only with him his wife also. Both believed in Latimore. Latimore does this so they could cover him and the church because Bishop Harris would not do it. Bishop Harris was hesitant to give his assistance because Latimore had decided to bypass the process of being properly ordained. Apostle and Prophetess Thompson are beautiful people, both inside and out. I would not trade their friendship and love for anything in the world. They loved and counseled us and treated us like their very own son and daughter. Apostle Thompson told Latimore that he would always be there for him whenever he needed help not to run the church but, to guide him along the way. I thought that was nice of him considering how Latimore's church got started. As by God, all things eventually come to light. I believe the Thompsons were hurt because it threatened their fifteen-year friendship with Bishop Harris. But still after it was all said and done, they stood by Latimore's side and helped me along in the process. They taught him how to bring me in as a partner of the church and not be in the background. With their help, that led to me becoming a Minster of the Lord's church. I told Latimore I would not accept it unless Apostle Thompson signed off on it because I do not play when it comes to order. I needed to know that this was God and not man, so I had to dig deep in my heart and soul with prayer, sincerity and know that this is God. So, I began to write out my first sermon and it was like the Heavens opened and dropped each word down into my spirit. What an amazing experience to hear God talking to you! I just said at that point God I surrender. Not, my will but your will God. And on July 12, 2014 I give my first sermon "There is a Season for Everything." My nerves are on edge, I am dropping my note cards and all, I got through it. When I finished, in that moment, I believed in me and knew within myself I was someone special in God's eyes. Despite it all he favored me. So, on that day I got ordained as Minister Marissa.

Prior to this we had a counseling session with the Thompson's to get our marriage in order because you cannot run a church with an out of order marriage. You cannot expect for it to go well and people to follow the leaders if they were not practicing what was being preached. Prophetess Thompson could see the hurt in me. A church needs a strong foundation to build a solid congregation. I really thought it would have been better had Latimore done it the right way and I was included in the process. Once again, the name of the game was Latimore's way. Always Latimore's game and his alone.

| 12 |

The ultimate betrayals

The job with the limo service leads to a promotion to fleet manager for Latimore. Things seem to be on the rise. He is making good money and our home situation is nice. I am not complaining because the money was good. I enjoyed our home; we were living in a four-level home on 2.5 acres. Five bedrooms with five bathrooms and the area was so serene. Olivia, my mother-in-law even liked it and said so. He had saved up and placed a two-thousand-dollar deposit towards purchasing it. He did this honestly. I did not have any inclination that is was not. The only draw was the commute. His drive was three hours daily, both ways on top of a 10-12-hour shift. Something was always happening with him coming home. Either he was falling asleep at the wheel and running off the road. Tires blowing out or the car breaking down. So, on Valentine's day while he was working, I went out and got him a travel car that was good on gas, one that I knew was safe and would get him to and from work. Being a concerned wife that is what I do. I make sure that my husband's wellbeing is always my first concern. Because of the commute, we agreed that he would stay there during the week and come home on the weekends. At first, he was coming home regularly, but something was off. You would think he would be glad to see us. Yet on the weekends he came, no attention was given to the kids or me. I am fixing meals and dressing in nice lingerie at times, making things romantic, so I thought. Yet this man is uncommunicative, distant once again. God does not allow things to stay in the dark too long.

One day he came home during the middle of the day nervous and wanting to have a drink and he says to me, "Marissa I just lost my job." I said, "you cannot be serious?" He goes on to say I do not know what the outcome is going to be, but I did something bad and our family could pay the price for it. I said "OK," but my dumb tail never asked why he lost his job. I just embraced him and told him that everything was going to be OK and left it as it was. A few months later he reveals what he did and shares it with his mom because we start to get information that people from the job was looking for him. Come to find out he has stolen money from his job. He was creating false invoices, redirecting funds to his companies, Install Masters and B & L Ducting. The latter was one of the companies that he started while on the current job, using that to take care of two households, ours, and his single life with Rochelle. I should have known something was up. I am flabbergasted beyond belief.

Everything begins to fall apart. He is drinking heavily. I get it. The stress of the situation had to be weighing heavy on him. These were felony charges. They were not completely going away no matter how hard we wished or prayed. The court case was playing out and everyone was on pins and needles. It was The fourth of July weekend July 5, 2012. The children were home and wanted to play. They were getting a little loud, so Latimore sent them out back to play. I agreed as I wanted to relax. I am watching one of my favorite shows, "Friends" in the bedroom. Meanwhile Latimore is in the kitchen, deep in thought, washing dishes. All the sudden he walks into the room, pulls my leg, and drags me to the end of the bed. I am thinking maybe we are about to have sex, but he begins beating me. I am immediately disoriented and just shocked. This is out of nowhere. All I could think was what did I do now? What did I do to deserve this? Please don't let my kids walk in on this?" He just kept beating and beating. The beating was so intense. I went from being dragged to the end of the bed, to being thrown on the floor. My head keeps hitting the floor like a drummer staying in beat. He picks me up and now my head is hitting the walls, the closet door of the bedroom. This was one time the strength of a man really outweighed me. I could not defend myself even if I tried. My head is hurting. I am seeing stars and then I see nothing at all. I black out becoming unconscious. I remember waking up, lying on the bed and Latimore is rocking and crying and apologizing profusely. He keeps saying "I don't know what came over me. I don't know what came over me." At that moment, honestly, I did not remember what happened to me, but I see the scratches and bruises on my neck. I start having flashbacks. I began putting the pieces together of what he did to me from his crying and apologizing. I knew at that moment; he totally lost control and did something bad to me. As with everything else, I let it go.

Now, I know what you are thinking. Why on God's earth, why IN HELL did not she call the police? Why didn't she have him arrested? My response "LOVE - COMPASSION." I loved him so much. The last thing he needed was another charge to add to the ones he already had pending. I just could not add the extra stress or years that he could be or would be incarcerated. Yes, I could have died that day, but the love I had for him ran so strong, so deep that at that point my life did not matter. Only he mattered. In that decision I knew I had lost complete control over me, my well-being. This was Latimore's world. Making sense of it was mute. I would not know until later just how much damage this beating did to me.

Still I stayed through the court case. The kids and I become homeless again because he surrendered everything to the job. He did not pay any bills so when it came time to reimburse the limo company, they kept all the monies from his paychecks. It did not matter that he had embarrassed me. I was determined to be there for him, through everything. His family had enough. They dropped him like a bad habit. Even after finding out about Rochelle, I stayed. July 14, 2014 my husband was sentenced. Here I am sitting in court with him and he is pleading to the judge.

First it was to assist us with housing. An eviction notice had been served. The judge told Latimore he should have taken care of this before final sentencing. He sounded like me, except I was a broken record. Up until that date I kept pleading with him to help us, to at least have some type of foundation, in other words some type of backup plan, for us to lean on while he was incarcerated. Instead he is paying seven thousand and some odd dollars towards restitution, instead of making sure we are okay. I thought "you are going to jail; you still must make restitution for what you stole, yet you take everything from us to at least survive for a minute. The judge sentences Latimore to three years without probation. His lawyer argues in hope that the judge will be lenient and reduce that due to time served. After listening to his lawyer, the judge changes his mind and gives Latimore, three years in jail and seven years on probation. In all a total of ten years.

I am not the one going to jail, yet I felt broken and defeated. Returning to a house, eviction notice served and only days to exit, I had no plan. Othello, a member of our church, came. He and Latimore were discussing the upkeep and status of the church during the trial. Othello comes and helps us pack our things. I do not know how much he knew about our current situation, but I was grateful for the help. His gesture did not stop there. He pulls out his credit card and tells me "whatever you need, you and your kids, food, drink, get what you need." I am floored, amazed, and just WOW! Who does that? Through the darkness and uncertainty surrounding me, here is a knight in shining armor riding up on a white horse. This man, another woman's husband, no strings attached showing kindness and compassion that I had never seen. Othello earned my respect and became a true friend of mine that day.

After the court case, losing everything, the beating I suffered before his sentencing, and his going to jail I was lost. I felt I was losing my mind and just did not know what to do. It was numbing. I was starting over again and trying to figure out my next steps. The kids and I moved to a hotel for about a week or two. After that, the Thompson's took us in for a while. I am still looking for housing, but everything now is upside down, large part due to Latimore. My initial plan was to stay in Virginia while Latimore was incarcerated. Throughout it all I was still supporting him. My mind, my body is constantly moving. I am not getting any sleep. I am doing everything I know to keep me and my kids afloat; I am still trying to keep my family together.

Before arriving at court that final day, Latimore hands me his personal items. We are were prayerful for a good outcome, but still there was probability that things would not go our way. After the judge handed down the sentence, I left the courthouse knowing now that he would not be coming home. First order of business was to get a power of attorney so I could handle Latimore's affairs on his behalf. You would think this would be his lowest point, that he would have time to reflect and make amends. Knowing he was isolated with no outs and plenty of time on his hands, I ask him to tell me the truth, "Have you over the years ever cheated on me?" He gave the typical Latimore response of no and continued to deny it. In my mind, I felt that he had slipped a couple of times, with the STD I contracted while pregnant with Muriel and the evidence I found on his phone during the incident at Walmart.

A few weeks pass and I get a letter from Latimore. He confesses to sleeping with six different women throughout our relationship. Six! My heart drops. I am crying and gasping for breath. I was so shaken. Shortly after reading the letter I get a call from Othello. He can tell immediately that something is wrong. He tells me to hold on, his lunch break is starting, and he is coming to me. He arrives and I am still inconsolable, unable to explain my hurt. I hand him the letter to read. Othello is visibly upset, calling Latimore "son of a bitch." "Why," he continues, "would he do that to you?" He spends his entire lunch break, one hour, trying to calm me down. "Right now," he tells me, "do what's best for you and your kids. Worry about here and now." Throughout this ordeal with Latimore, I found that I could really count on Othello. He was a great friend. We had been spending time together with him helping me find temporary shelter, moving our things we had left to storage and breaking down the church Latimore had started. His wife was not living in Virginia at the time, so we were leaning on each other during a difficult time. We became intimate during this time. Two wrongs do not make it right, I know that. With everything that was going on, my intentions were not to get back at Latimore for cheating. I was physically and emotionally depleted. I needed love at that moment. Everything was falling apart around me and Othello the gentleman, the knight who rode in on his white horse, was there. After all the hell Latimore put me through, I will always cherish that moment.

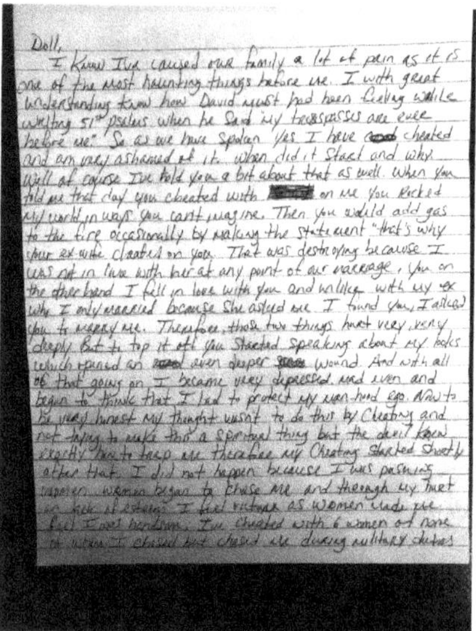

Doll,

I know I've caused our family a lot of pain as it is one of the most haunting things before me. I with great understanding know how David must had been feeling while writing 51st psalms when he said my trespasses are ever before me." So as we have spoken yes I have cheated and am very ashamed of it. When did it start and why will of course I've told you a bit about that as well. When you told me that day you cheated with ███ on me you rocked my world in ways you can't imagine. Then you would add gas to the fire occasionally by making the statement "that's why your ex-wife cheated on you. That was destroying because I was not in love with her at any point of our marriage, you on the other hand I fell in love with you and unlike with my ex who I only married because she asked me I found you, I asked you to marry me. Therefore, those two things hurt very, very deeply. But to top it off you started speaking about my looks which opened an even deeper wound. And with all of that going on I became very depressed and even and began to think that I had to protect my man-hood ego. Now to be very honest my thought wasn't to do this by cheating and not trying to make this a spiritual thing but the devil knew exactly how to trap me therefore my cheating started shortly after that. I did not happen because I was pushing women women began to chase me and through my hurt in pride of esteem I feel victim as women made me feel I was handsome. I've cheated with 6 women not none of whom I chased but chased me during military duties

Pleading for another chance

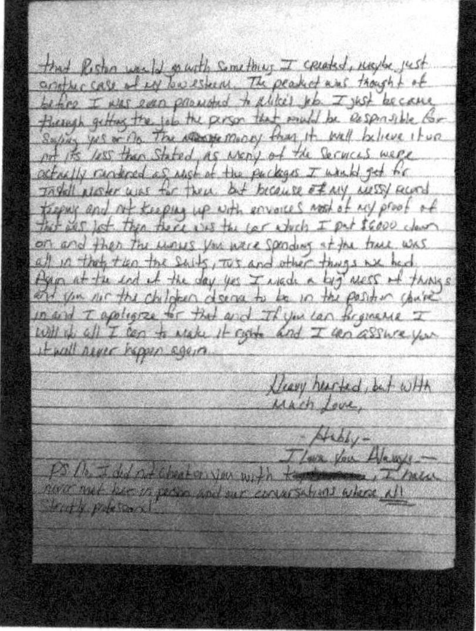

I took a little time to get my mind together. One of Latimore's flings I found was still on-going. Rochelle. Wanting to know more, I contacted the limo service where Latimore had worked and inquired about the auto part company, they did service with. Getting the information, I contacted Rochelle and as politely as I could asked about their relationship. She went on to tell me that it started as casual flirting. She knew he was married and a father. It did not stop her or his pursuit of her. He came and she did not deny him or his money. She goes on to say that with his help of five hundred dollars monthly, she and her son moved into a new apartment. Monday through Thursday he was living with her, coming home to his family on the weekends. She heard every argument we had on the phone. Claiming he had to work on the 4th of July, he goes and hangs out with her, meeting her family like they were a couple. Rochelle then has the gall to say that at one point she wanted to come see me and tell me what was happening. I told her "be glad you didn't because the outcome wasn't going to be in your favor. One of us, and it was not going to be me would not be returning home, point blank!

She agreed commenting, "I knew then I did not want any part of you. When he came to me after your incident at Walmart. If you could do that to a 6'1 dude, who am I?" SLAM ON THE BREAKS! After the Walmart incident, he went running to her? Hold up! What? This woman was supposed to be Donald's girlfriend; that is what he said then right? THE DARK SKIN WOMAN IN THE SEE-THROUGH WHITE OUTFIT ON HIS PHONE! He was seeing her then and had continued up through the trial? Oh, hell no! You can imagine the anger and hurt I felt at that point. I told her "you are somebody just as well. I did not deserve this from either of you, but you did it anyway. You stole from me. You stole from his children playing this game you played. His kids are innocent in this. Karma happens and both of you will pay in the end."

In September, my sister Maxine says "Marissa, just come home." I move back to her house for about three weeks before moving to Garrett County, Maryland into a shelter. Still I am working, hustling trying my best to have some type of normalcy for us. Yet none of this prepared me for what happened next. December 4, 2014 started as an ordinary day. Nothing since that day will ever be ordinary for me again.

| 13 |

December 4, 2014

Maxine's story

"My sister was admitted to the hospital. I get there and they tell me she is in critical condition. I ask them how is this possible? What happen to her? They tell me she had multiple seizures and they are trying their best to stabilize her. The doctors skirt around asking questions, trying to deny or confirm their suspicions. They inform us that there is quite a bit of scar tissue around her brain from an injury. They did not want to say from abuse, it could have been from an auto accident or something else, but it was becoming clear to me that it was. I knew. Like my sister, I too had been in abusive situations and saw all the signs. When Marissa first met Latimore, I cautioned her to take time, just take some time to really get to know him. Everything was moving so fast. She is pregnant and married to him within a couple of months. The constant moving. I did not know the exact extent, but I knew something was amiss. He was isolating her from her family so he could do what he wanted. The fights, the arguments, each becoming more intense than the last. The signs were there. The turtlenecks and long sleeve shirts to hide the scratches, bruises. The excuses she made for him. Now I am here praying, scared shitless while she is fighting for her life. My mind flashes back to two weeks before Latimore was sentenced. Before the sentencing even occurred, I talked to Latimore about the court case he was going through, and I told him what God had given me to tell him. God told me if you tell the truth about everything that he would make your burden easy.

That Sunday Marissa wore a turtleneck to church. She mentioned that there was an incident on Saturday, but she did not go into a lot of details, only that it was different than the other times. I asked her what happened, but she said she could not remember; only from his apologies that he had hit and choked her. Slamming her head repeatedly into the floor and walls of the closet doors. They finally get my sister stabilized. I leave the hospital and immediately they are calling me back because she's had another one," Maxine tells me. I blame Latimore completely. In the worst moment he became the biggest bully. He chose to remain in control instead of letting God taking control of the situation. His actions alone caused my sister to be in this place. For the rest of her life she will have to deal with having unexpected seizures that one day may kill her. But I know her to be a fighter and you will get through this and through it all.

Dad's story

"I'm at home visiting my girlfriend in Baltimore. The date is December 4th and I get this call from the hospital. I confirm that she is. My blood starts to grow cold. Someone, I cannot remember if it was a male or female voice, told me that my daughter has been admitted. She is in critical condition and I need to get there as soon as possible. Her condition is grave, and it is possible she is not going to make it. "What a minute? What?", I interrupt. What is going on? What's happens to my daughter? That's my oldest daughter. I need to know what's going on with her. Somebody needs to tell me right now, what is going on." They inform me that she is had a seizure and that they are unable to stabilize her, and I just need to get there as quickly as I can. So, I get in my car. I get on the road. My other daughter Diamond shows up along with me and, I am crying all the way up to Garrett County. I am crying and praying, and I am crying, and I am praying. I get to the hospital and the lady from the shelter tells me that my grandson Cephas found his mother shaking uncontrollably. To see my baby with all the tubes and everything. I hear the doctors asking if I am aware of any accidents that she had that would have caused the swelling of her brain from a fractured skull. Um, I just I know immediately who put her there. His name is Latimore. Latimore, he put her there and I am angry. First time he put his hands on my child I remember going to the house and telling him I am her father. I am her father – nobody, nobody puts their hand on my child but me. Keep your hands off my daughter. Do not hit her anymore, but that first time it wasn't the last. Every time he did it, I'm calling the police, but there's little that I can do as her father because she's not reporting him. The police tell me Sir there is nothing that we can do unless she reports it. So, I am there with my child, seven days. For seven days, I am crying, and I am praying that my child is going to be okay. The first few days were a blur because they just kept trying to stabilize my child. She died four times and they brought her back from death. Each time her heart stopped I felt I was going to die right along with her. She died four times and for seven days I stayed right there by her side. I would not leave her, I could not. That's my baby."

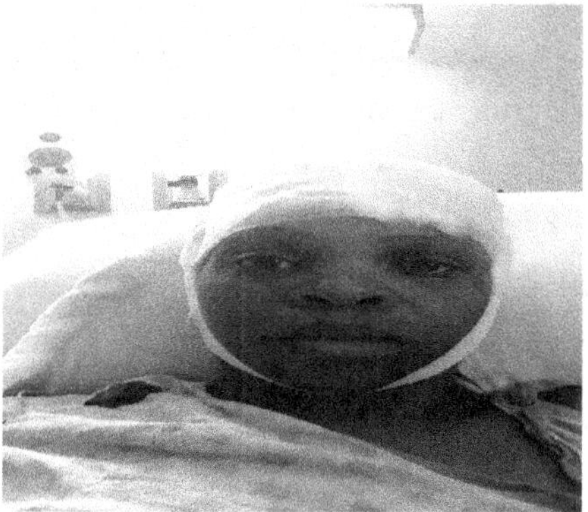

After a seizure attack

My story

I have heard the stories of what happened that day. My memories are sporadic. What I remember is not much. The kids and I were living at the shelter in Garrett County. I got off from work; I had a headache.

I really was not feeling that well, but I kept pushing myself because I needed to do what I needed to do to for me and my children. I get back to the shelter. I remember thinking I had to get the kids ready for school the next day. It was Thursday, but I figured I would just lay down for a few minutes to catch my breath. My head was pounding from a bad headache. I had just got off the phone with Latimore. He told me that the judge denied his request to be released early. I told him okay and that I needed to get off the phone. The next thing I know it is several days later. I am waking up in the hospital. I stayed there from December 4th to January 7th.

Hearing this from Maxine and my father was hard. I finally realized that I was not the only one going through the abuse I endured. She knew first-hand and to watch me experience the same, I cannot imagine the pain she felt. Domestic violence affects the entire family, from the victim to their children and other family members watching them, and many not even knowing the abuse is happening. In the moment I did not want to hear that Latimore was not the perfect soulmate for me. Nobody could tell me anything, nothing. I was in denial. No amount of words from Maxine, my dad, nobody was going to sway me, or move me to leave him. Nobody. I loved him. I knew once he was out of jail that we would have another chance to start over. I believed it. Nothing and nobody would convince

I do not remember much about the month I spent in the hospital. I know that they were looking after my kids. Maxine asked if I wanted my children to go with her. I said no. I wanted them to stay near me. They (my family and the shelter) arranged for a foster family, close by, to care for them. I have a vague memory of my father and my sisters being there, but everything was such a blur. I am just going by the story told to me afterwards. They told me that Cephas found me on the bed shaking uncontrollably and my eyes were white with no pupil showing. He ran to the woman that was running the shelter and they quickly called 911. They told me that I died. I was resuscitated four times. So, the children came back from foster care once I go back to the shelter on January 7th. I was so blessed because the foster care mother was one of the ladies from our church. She took my kids in and my church family, Loch Lynn Church of God, was there for me from the start and helped nurse me back. They helped me get back up on my feet. I would not trade them for the world. They were a true blessing and miracle to me, along with the Dove Shelter. It took me so long to have some semblance of a normal life, but I knew my life would never ever be the same, that the seizures, epilepsy, would be with me until I died. When I got out the hospital, I was all set to move into my new apartment in Garrett County. Weak as I was, I had to do same traveling. I made three trips. First, I went to Baltimore, Maryland to my family to show them what God had given me back, my life. It was an awesome move of God in my sister Dorine's house that day. I believe each person came to receive and expect God to move. But most of all they wanted to see the Miracle that God did at that point in my life.

Secondly, I went to Newport News, Virginia to see Othello to let him know I was ok. When I arrived at the hotel, the first thing he did was embrace me. We just stood there for the longest holding each other. Despite the distance we had remained friends, he was and still is my best friend. My move to Garrett County, trying to rebuild a life for me and my children kept me pretty busy, with little time to connect with my friend. We had so much to catch up on. As always, Othello patiently listened as I told him everything about that day, I had the seizures, the doctor's findings and everything I went through to recover. Seeing me and hearing my story, he could not believe what Latimore had done. He was beside himself. I could feel his anger. It was raw and his face was etched in pain and fury. I could see his emotions, him grappling with what I now have to endure for the rest of my life. Through it all, he never felt sorry for me. All he wanted was for me to be okay. I will always respect him for that. As close as we were, I was just not ready for anything else but friendship. He was still married, and I respected that. We ended the meeting with promises to stay in touch with each other.

Finally, I made the visit to see Latimore; it took all of me. It took a lot of nerve and will power but I wanted him to see me. To show him what he did to me - I had lost weight, my hair was coming out. I was unable to walk without the assistance of a walker or my children assisting me. I also had the assistance of a seizure dog. I had a nurse that came around the clock to make sure that I was no longer having seizures on a regular basis. I am on seizure medication. I could not drive; I could not work but I was determined that I had to get back to some sense of normalcy because my kids needed me. They needed me. I was determined that I would be able to walk and take care of myself again.

Only Latimore did not see it that way at all. All I got was a blank stare, like nothing was wrong. He did not ask about my hair. He did not ask why I was so thin. The walker sitting beside me was invisible to him. Squaring my shoulders and gathering my nerves, I told him about the seizures. I told him the story that Maxine and my daddy relayed to me about how many times I died. This MAN sitting across from me had the gall to say that old childhood injuries I endured caused my seizures. CHILDHOOD INJURIES. Fifteen years later, childhood injuries caused my seizures. NO REMORSE AT ALL. NONE. He simply sat there and denied his role, his part in it all.

| 14 |

Getting Over and Moving on

It is six months after Latimore has been incarcerated. I was the only one reaching out, making sure he had funds in his account to purchase items in jail, and making sure that he could call by paying for Home-WAV, a conferencing service that jails use. I was the one that would risk my life, driving through bad snowstorms getting into accidents, to visit and bring the kids so he would still be a part of their life. As far as visits and mail, the Thompson's came a few times and wrote letters. His brother Martin did a few HomeWAV video chats. Brigette and Mr. Keith sent a card. Incarceration is shameful and awfully expensive on the family providing extra care and needs of the prisoner. But, little old me wanting him to him to have what he needed and then some. That is just the person that I am. After years of emotional and physical abuse, that last beating took more from me than I realized. I started wondering was it worth it to stay. I was hurt, angry. I had every right to be. This man continued to humiliate me over and repeatedly. I loved him but the damage from the seizures was just too much. I always prided myself on the fact that if I got knocked down, I was found a way back. Not knowing if I am going to have a seizure my children are constantly vigilant to watch over me, knowing what signs to look for in case they need to call 911. The recovery period after having one, days of slurred speech, waiting for my mind to reconnect with my body so I can walk, without having to roll myself because I have no lower body strength to stand and walk. Having to wear a helmet to protect my skull and brain. My cognitive skills, trying to write, remember simple things can be exhausting. This is what Latimore did to me.

While he was in prison, I had two extra-marital affairs. The first with Othello which last two years. Yes, his wife was still in the picture, but they were going through things. The compassion and tenderness that Othello showed me was everything that had been missing from my relationship with my husband. The intimacy between us was over the moon. I had never experienced love like this and yes, I fell in love. It was so deep. I gave Othello everything that I had given Latimore, my heart, my mind, and soul. It was wonderful to be loved without all the baggage that Latimore had given me. After two years, we fell apart, but my heart now belonged to Othello.

After that affair, I was attending church at New Genesis Total Praise Center. I was reconnecting with my spirituality and I felt that change was coming my way. Most of the anger and pain I had been feeling was starting to dissipate. One Sunday morning, I was in the pulpit singing during praise and worship, when a gentleman walked in with his four children. Our eyes met. The attraction was instant and mutual. We connected through our daughters, who talk to each other on a regular basis when they see one another in church. Xavier was exceptionally smooth. He had a way with the ladies. Like Latimore, he had a way with words. But unlike Latimore, he knew how to treat a lady and I took comfort it that. I ended up getting drawn into the situation mostly because of his daughters, I came to care for them deeply, but I was also getting the attention I felt I needed. However, I was not getting the honesty that comes with it. Elders in the church were trying to steer me in the right direction, but I was being disobedient. Needless to say, I discovered that Xavier was still married. He had filed for divorce, but it was not final. Upon learning this, I was not ready to get caught up with another married man.

January 31, 2017 Latimore was scheduled to be released from prison. I left Maryland early that morning to pick him up. I wanted to be sure I was there on time. The night before I said my goodbyes to Xavier and his daughters. I had decided to give my marriage another try.

Finding beauty after the seizures

On the way back to Garrett County, we chatted. The conversation reminded me of the beginning of our relationship, good and stimulating. We get home and have sex for the first time in a few years. All the flashbacks start roaring back; the yelling, pushing, fighting back just to end the arguments, the fear of being beaten. All the stress leads to me having another seizure. Latimore calls out to Cephas "come help your mom." He did not attempt to help or ask any questions. When it was over, he acted like it never happened. In the immortal words of Fred Sanford "this big dummy" acted like a true dummy. There had been many moments between us, but that one? In that crisis, my life possibly on the line, where was his compassion? We stood before God and vowed to take care of each other, "for better or worse". Where was that compassionate man now?

For the first time, more than my body is uncomfortable. My spirit and my soul is uneasy. After a few days I call Xavier to get a male's perspective, another point of view. He's not happy stating "I haven't heard from you in a few days and now you're calling to talk about your husband?" He begins to put the facts together, as I had not told him when Latimore was coming home. So now I am seeing Xavier again and home with my husband. I begin to feel uncomfortable, with both of us being married to someone else. I made the decision to break it off and completely commit to my marriage.

Although I did not want to be around Latimore physically, I continued to help him get on his feet. I helped him get bonded and found him a place in Hagerstown. While he was there, I found out he is seeing another woman. Wow! Here we go again, on repeat mode. The same old cycle, MO with him. Still determined to make a fresh start, I convince him to move home, back to Baltimore, MD. I had returned to going to church, which he had an issue with, partly because of the church he founded while in Virginia. I had no intentions of starting a new church with him and that did not go over well. Our relationship was still on rocky roads when we moved again, this time to Frederick, Maryland.

On December 4, 2017 I filed for divorce. I was spending a lot of time with my church family and Latimore had paid for me to go on a seven-day cruise with them. I was looking forward to spending some time alone and getting a new perspective on my marriage. Xavier drove me down to the Florida port along with members of my family, my sister Maxine and my niece Missy were also going.

None of that mattered to Latimore. In his mind, I was going to have another extra marital affair. There was no changing his mind that this was a church event and having sex with anybody was the furthest thing on my mind. While on the cruise, I called home to check in, but Latimore's mood had not changed one bit. He was still so angry and bitter. The conversation did not go well at all. On the last day of the cruise, I had decided that hell or high water, Latimore and the kids were my life, my family and I was determined to make us whole.

My mind made up; Xavier is at the port to give me a ride back home. He knew that I had decided to return to my marriage and was going to tell Latimore as soon as I arrived home. Latimore, however, had other plans. While I was on the cruise, he was trying to set up house with another female. I truly believe that Latimore cannot take care of himself. He has to have a woman in the picture to prop him up. Everything he told the woman was to make me look like the monster; what I was or was not doing on the cruise. Instead of her minding her business, he said she sought out him out. And Latimore allow it to go down because his old habits never change. Instead, of him trying to see what was going to happen with our relationship it was move on time once again. And like I said it does not take long for him. So, when we get back from the cruise Xavier and I walk over to the car to let Latimore know my decision. I believe that Xavier felt like he won this battle but at the end Latimore forfeit by the shaking of hands with Xavier and telling him "man, you can have her." Latimore said his piece and I called him and told to get out my house. The rest is history. That was my last encounter with my husband on December 17, 2017.

After that occurred, I put me and our children in intense therapy and counseling. Something I asked Latimore to do to help get our marriage back on track many times throughout our marriage. He vehemently refused. He viewed counseling as a sign of weakness. Counseling does not make you weak, only stronger. For me and my children, counseling helped us build a stronger foundation. Our communication skills are better. It helped us set goals and most importantly not dwell on the past and the pain we endured. For more than a year, I had four sessions a week. My children had sessions not only at school, but also home. Despite all that was said, some weeks later I saw him in my neighborhood. I decided to file for an exporta order of protection. Due to his previous flare-ups I was fearful of him becoming violent and I just refused to take anymore. It did not matter to him. He continued to gloat and throw his new woman up in my face on Facebook where he would connect with the other woman, touting all our business to her. I really did not know what he thought would come of it. Maybe he thought he would get some sympathy. Maybe he thought she would see me as a liar or evil. Turns out that it did not take her long to see him for who he really was. She called to apologize. I accepted. What happened next though I was not expecting. I gained a spiritual friend, sister, and mentor in a woman he thought would break my pride once again.

It took two men, and his immediate repeat of this is the Latimore way of life, to convince me what my family had been trying so hard to do. I finally came to the realization that loving someone does not mean you become their physical punching bag. Love should not leave you emotionally scarred or physically damaged. Love does have two-way communication, ups and downs not one-sided barriers hell bent on destroying the other's compassion.

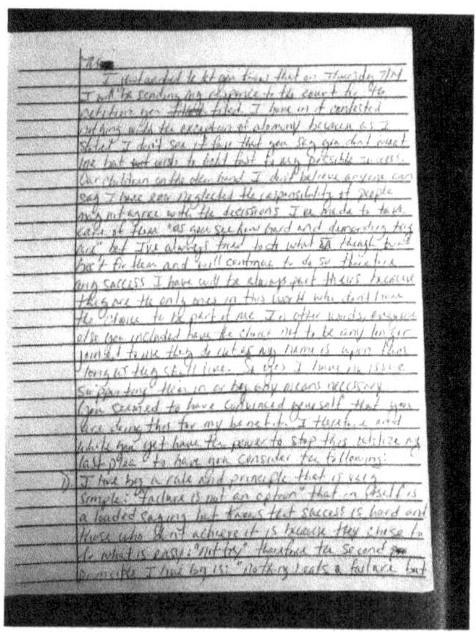

Too little too late

Too little too late

February 16, 2018 our divorce became final. I tried being his friend for our children's sake, but like our marriage he was not interested in moving forward like two normal human beings. Like his previous relationships, he turned the page. Because I left, now his kids no longer matter. See when he came out jail, I had everything that was taken from me, replaced by my hard work of rebuilding on my own. He left us like discarded trash to fend for ourselves.

The year is now 2018. Othello and I found our way back to each other. With my divorce from Latimore in my rearview mirror, I am finally learning how to be content on my own. March 26, 2018 Othello reaches out on Facebook asking me to contact him. I did not respond at first. He persisted asking "where is my friend." I was hesitant to respond because of everything that I had been through, but my heart would not allow me not to call and at least say hello. After receiving couple more text messages from him, I called and said, "what do you want?" The last time we spoke he was still married. My next question was "are you still married?". He heard my divorce was finalized and wanted to know how I was doing. He told me he had gotten a divorce in 2016 and was content being a single man. He said he was relieved that I was able to move on. He thought about me and the kids often and wondered how I was adjusting to my health situation. I must admit it was nice to just have someone there to just be my friend. Here we both are single. This was our chance to see if our relationship could grow into something more. Our friendship continued to blossom and on March 8, 2020 I agreed to become his wife. I am truly happy.

I am working on a career path that I love and raising Cephas and Muriel. I have visitation to see Theo anytime I want. Are we still battered and scarred? Yes, but we are in a much better, stronger place. I continue to have seizures. I take the medication and stay cautious, but I am living for every minute. I take nothing for granted; life is way too short I know that. Never did I imagine that part of my life story, my journey would be so dramatic, filled with so much turmoil. I hope that Latimore can find the peace that he has been missing. I wish him well and hope that he can find happiness in his new marriage.

If there is one thing I know for sure, there is a God. He watched over me and continues to keep me in his graces. I have learned to fight for me, for my kids, and for my happiness and I refuse to let anyone ever hurt me that way again. I am a strong black woman on the move. I plotted my three-year goal for 2020-2023 because I took a stand to save my life. In closing I ask to you consider this. Please, whether you are a woman or man, DO NOT take nothing off a person that is not worthy of your love, sincerity, and affection. If they cannot love or like you for who you are, keep it moving because they will not be there to support you fully in your walk, your journey, your purpose in life.

Did you know

Truths from the National Coalition Against Domestic Violence (ncadv.org)

1. Almost twenty people are physically violated every sixty seconds
2. Domestic violence happens to men and women
3. Physical violence no matter how casual is common. One out of every four women, and one out of every nine men experience some type of intimate physical abuse.
4. Domestic abuse can leave long/short term health effects such as post-traumatic stress disorder (PTSD), emotional and neurological disorders, anxiety, depression, sexually transmitted diseases, chronic pain, and disabilities.

Signs of domestic abuse

1. Coerced or controlling behavior
2. Slapping, shoving, pushing
3. Stalking
4. Showing an intent to slap, choke or push in a menacing manner.

ABOUT THE AUTHOR

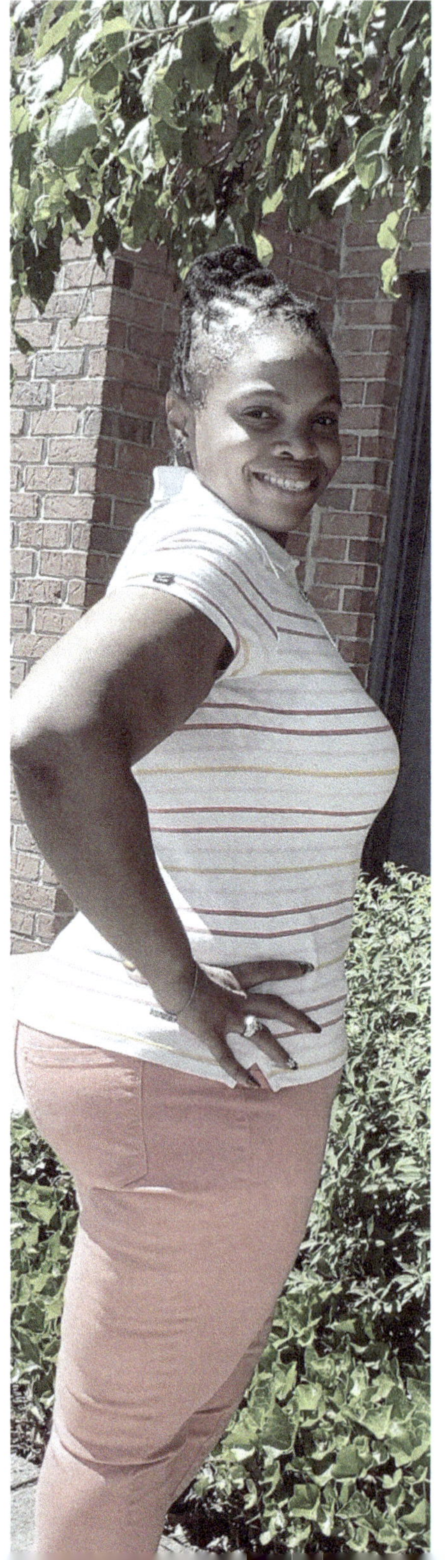

Mia W. Jones was born and raised in Baltimore, Maryland. A loving wife and mother of three children, she is a survivor of domestic abuse and an advocate for women and men traumatized by or going through domestic violence. She is working hard on her three-year plan to secure a better future for her and the wonderful family that she has now. She is sharing her story in hopes to raise awareness and empower to other women and men on domestic violence. She is asking that you share and let others know there is help in their communities if they need assistance. Please feel free to email her if you need help at walkinginpurpose228@gmail.com She will be sure to point you in the right direction and help if she can. Also, she is available for workshops and seminars.

Thank you in advance for all your love and support.